# Magic
## Animal Friends

For Skye Sankey,
the most beloved

## Special thanks to Valerie Wilding

ORCHARD BOOKS

First published in Great Britain in 2018 by The Watts Publishing Group

1 3 5 7 9 10 8 6 4 2

Text copyright © Working Partners Ltd 2018
Illustrations copyright © Working Partners Ltd 2018
Series created by Working Partners Ltd

A CIP catalogue record for this book is available from the British Library.

ISBN 978 1 40834 712 6

Printed in Great Britain

MIX
Paper from
responsible sources
FSC
www.fsc.org     FSC® C104740

The paper and board used in this book are made from wood from responsible sources

Orchard Books
An imprint of Hachette Children's Group
Part of The Watts Publishing Group Limited
Carmelite House, 50 Victoria Embankment, London EC4Y 0DZ

An Hachette UK Company
www.hachette.co.uk
www.hachettechildrens.co.uk

# Daisy Tappytoes
# Dares to Dance

Daisy Meadows

ORCHARD

Toadstool Glade

Bluebell
Brook

Friendship
Tree

Babblehop Barn

Billy Stoutfoot's
Cobblers

Nibblesqueak Bakery

Boggit
Swamp

The Whizzpaws'
Tower

Grizelda's
Tower

Friendship Forest
Weather Station

Map of Friendship Forest

Can you keep a secret? I thought you could!

Then I'll tell you about an enchanted wood.

It lies through the door in the old oak tree,

Let's go there now - just follow me!

We'll find adventure that never ends,

And meet the Magic Animal Friends!

Love,
Goldie the Cat

# Contents

## CHAPTER ONE

# A Golden Visitor

Jess Forester woke suddenly. For a

moment, she wondered where she was.

Then she remembered. She was having

a sleepover at her best friend Lily Hart's

house! But what had woken her?

*Tap tap tap tap!*

Jess poked the bundle of covers in the

 9

next bed. "Wake up!"

Lily's sleepy face appeared. She opened one eye.

"Listen," said Jess.

*Tap tap tap tap!*

"I think it's coming from outside," Jess said. "But what could it be?"

Lily sat up.

"I think I know! It must be the woodpecker Mum and Dad have been looking after.

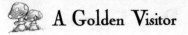 

They said he was feeling better." She jumped out of bed. "Let's get dressed and go and see him!"

*Tap tap tap tap tap!*

Jess laughed. "He definitely sounds better!"

Minutes later, the girls ran down the garden towards Helping Paw Wildlife Hospital. It was run by Mr and Mrs Hart inside their barn. Lily and Jess loved all animals, and adored helping to look after the patients.

Nearby was the aviary – a huge tent made of netting, big enough for birds to fly around in. Jess spotted a jackdaw with a bandaged leg, a tiny sparrow and a robin with missing tail feathers.

*Tap tap tap tap tap!*

"There's the woodpecker." Lily pointed to a green bird with bandaged wings. Its red-topped head bobbed back and forth as it knocked at a tree stump with its long, strong beak.

Jess crouched down close to the netting. "You'll soon be flying again, little one," she said softly.

"Let's see how the rabbits are doing," suggested Lily.

They found two baby bunnies outside their hutch, sniffing the morning air with their snuffly noses. Jess was leaning into the run to stroke them, when her eye was caught by a flash of gold beside the hay store.

"Goldie!" she cried, and dashed across the grass.

Lily's heart leapt as she followed Jess.
Goldie was a beautiful cat with sparkling
green eyes, and the girls' special friend.
She was from a magical place called
Friendship Forest, where the animals
talked and lived in pretty little cottages
and dens. Goldie often took the girls there
for amazing adventures!

She curled around the girls' legs,
purring. Lily stroked her soft golden fur.
"Are you taking us to Friendship Forest?"

With a joyful mew, Goldie darted
towards Brightley Stream, at the bottom
of the Harts' garden.

 14

The girls raced after
her, over the stream's
stepping stones and into Brightley
Meadow. Goldie headed for a dead-
looking tree. As she reached it, it
burst into life, sprouting bright green
leaves. Pink and yellow honeysuckle
scrambled between the branches,
while plump, sleepy bumblebees
visited the flowers. In the lush
grass below, cheeky

red-breasted chaffinches hopped among scarlet poppies, trilling their happy song.

When Goldie touched the tree with her paw, two words appeared in the bark.

"Friendship Forest!" the girls read aloud, and suddenly, there was a door in the tree trunk. Lily reached for its leaf-shaped handle, and opened it. A beautiful golden light shone out.

The girls squeezed each other's hands excitedly, and followed Goldie inside. Their skin tingled all over, as if they were swimming in a fizzy drink, and they knew that they were shrinking a little.

 16

When the light faded, they found themselves in a sunlit forest glade. The air was filled with the delicious scents of lemon berries and chocolate cherry blossoms.

Waiting for the girls, standing almost as tall as their shoulders, was Goldie. Her glittery scarf fluttered in the breeze as she reached out to hug them.

"It's great to be back in Friendship Forest!" cried Jess.

Goldie was now able to speak to them in her soft voice. "I'm so happy you're here." Her scarf flapped over her face. She

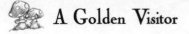 

pulled it away, laughing.

"It's still windy in the forest," Lily said anxiously. "Is Grizelda up to her tricks again?"

Grizelda was a horrible witch who desperately wanted to get rid of all the animals and keep Friendship Forest for herself. On the girls' last visit, Grizelda had released a wind sprite called Gale, who had created powerful, dangerous whirlwinds that almost destroyed the animals' homes. Luckily the girls had stopped the witch's nasty plan.

"Don't worry," Goldie said. "No one's

seen Grizelda lately." She took their hands in her soft paws. "I've brought you today for something really exciting – a musical show at Harmony Hall. Would you like to come?"

Lily and Jess grinned at each other. "Yes, please!" they cried.

CHAPTER TWO

# Disaster at Harmony Hall

Goldie and the girls hurried through the forest. They joined scurrying hamsters, bouncy lambs and tumbling puppies, all heading for Harmony Hall. Millie Picklesnout the piglet snorted with laughter as she chased her brother, Benji,

 21

and butterflies giggled as they were
tossed about by the breeze. Hopping frogs
overtook Mrs Twinkletail the mouse, who
was pushing her babies in the double-
decker buggy invented for her by Mr
Cleverfeather the owl.

Soon they reached a clearing and
Goldie pulled aside a curtain of glossy
green ivy. "Welcome back to Harmony
Hall!"

The outdoor theatre was filled with

excited animals, all sitting on benches of
shiny, smooth pink stone that glistened
in the sunlight. Curtains of woven vines
hung across the stage, where a large
orange flower seemed to be growing on a
tall green stem.

"What a pretty flower," said Jess.

"That's Mr Cleverfeather's Marigold
Microphone," said Goldie.

"Amazing!" said Lily, her eyes wide. Mr
Cleverfeather was always inventing just

the right thing for whatever the animals in Friendship Forest needed, and a microphone that looked like a flower was perfect for Harmony Hall.

"Lily! Jess! Goldie!" Mr Littleleap the goat ranger from Magic Mountain waved his hat to attract their attention. "I've saved seats for you, behind us."

"Thank you, Mr Littleleap!" called Jess.

The friends made their way to the seats and found themselves next to two smiling deer.

"I'm Mr Tappytoes," said one. His chestnut-coloured fur was dappled with

24

cream spots. He had polished antlers and a waistcoat of golden-brown beech leaves. "We know who you are, Lily and Jess! You're wonderful friends to all the animals in Friendship Forest. It's nice to finally meet you."

"Lovely to meet you, too," said Jess.

"And I'm Mrs Tappytoes," said the other deer. She wore a necklace made from buttercups and clover. She fidgeted with excitement. "Our daughter Daisy will be so excited that you're here. She's doing a solo tap dance in the show!" she said.

"Ooh, we can't wait to see her," said Lily.

As Mrs Tappytoes took a handkerchief from her handbag, the girls caught sight of a folded piece of paper. It looked like a map.

Jess glanced at Lily. They'd seen something like that before. "Is that one of the Friendship Forest maps?" she asked.

"Oh, yes," said Mrs Tappytoes. "It shows

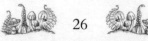

the northern part of Friendship Forest. Our family protects this map and we never let it out of our sight – it's why I've brought it to the show."

The girls weren't surprised to hear this. If something bad happened to the map, the same bad thing would happen to the forest. They remembered when the map of the southern part of the forest was ripped in two – a huge chasm had appeared in the forest floor, and to make it disappear they'd had to put the map back together.

With a clatter of tiny hooves, an adorable young fawn rushed towards Mr

and Mrs Tappytoes. She was the colour of soft caramel, with creamy spots.

"Mum! Dad!" she cried. "I'm so excited about the show!" She noticed Jess and Lily, and her long eyelashes fluttered. "Wowee! I've always wanted to meet you two!"

Lily grinned. "You must be Daisy Tappytoes."

The fawn beamed. "I am!" She danced a few steps on her slender legs. *Tap tap tippy-tippy tap tap.* "I've got to go backstage now. I'm on first!"

"Good luck!" called the girls.

Daisy danced off, and a few minutes later, the curtain opened. There she was, wearing a glittery silver tiara, and four matching shiny tap shoes.

The crowd cheered as she began her dance. Her red shoes clicked on the stage as she twirled and shuffled back and forth. *Tappety tappety tap-tap-tap* … It was all in perfect time to the music.

Suddenly, Daisy squealed and ran behind the curtain.

To Jess and Lily's horror, an orb of greenish-yellow light floated on to the stage. The audience gasped.

"Grizelda!" cried Jess.

The animals cowered in their seats as the orb burst into a shower of smelly sparks.

There stood the horrible witch, her green hair swirling like mouldy worms around her bony face. She wore a purple tunic over skinny black trousers and spiky boots.

Jess leapt to her feet. "What do you want, Grizelda?"

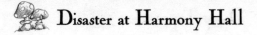 

The witch glared. "I'm getting rid of all
the nasty animals, once and for all!"

She clapped twice, and a tiny bottle
with a purple cork appeared in her hands.
Colours swirled inside it – grey, green,
purple and blue.

Jess and Lily knew that inside the
bottle were four sprites who were helping
Grizelda. Each lived on one of the four
winds.

Grizelda shook the bottle and four little
round faces pressed against the glass. They
stared out with large, shining eyes.

The witch's lip curled as she uncorked

the bottle.

*Pop!*

"Haa!" she shrieked. "Puff, Puff! Do as you must!"

The blue sprite slithered out of the bottle and began to grow. His deep blue body became paler and almost see-through. When he was as big as the girls, he puffed out his cheeks and gave a piercing whistle.

*Peeeeeeeeeeeeeeeep!*

Everyone yelped and covered their ears.

"That hurts!" Lucy Longwhiskers the rabbit whimpered, folding her ears down.

 32

"Haf haf!"
Puff laughed.
"I'm the loudest, best
whistler ever—"

"Pipe down about
your silly whistle,"
Grizelda snapped.

"But everyone will
want to hear how amazing
my whistle is," Puff protested.

Grizelda glared at him and stamped
her foot. "Begin the plan now!" she said.

"OK," Puff said crossly. He puffed out his cheeks and sent a whistling blast of wind straight at Daisy's parents.

The wind snatched up Mrs Tappytoes' handbag and pulled out the map.

"No!" Goldie cried. She leaped up and tried to catch it, but the map flew into the air and over the heads of the watching animals. It flapped towards Grizelda, who reached out and grabbed it.

Jess gasped. Lily's hands clamped over her mouth in horror.

If Grizelda had the map, who knew what she'd do to Friendship Forest?

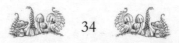

34

## CHAPTER THREE

# Moo Moo Milkshakes

Grizelda held up a grey finger. She scratched the map with a long, pointy black nail, chanting:

*"With my fingernail so black,*

*Friendship Forest I attack!*

*All these pictures quickly switch*

 35

*To make it fitting for
a witch!"*

Lily and Jess stared in shock
as the sparkling pink benches
turned grey and dull. Thorny
vines burst from the ground and
animals scurried away, squealing
and tripping over each other. Mrs
Tappytoes jumped up in shock, and a
piglet squealed, "What's happening?"
But before anyone could
answer, Puff whistled into the
microphone. *Peeeeeeeeep!* The
ghastly whistle blasted across

the hall and out over the forest.

All the animals covered their ears once more and a baby lamb started crying.

Jess and Lily crept to the side of the stage. Now they could see that Grizelda had drawn thorny vines and dollops of muck over the map, covering the images of cottages, trees, even Spelltop School. Dirt and vines continued to spread across the theatre.

"Oh no!" Lily whispered. "Remember, whatever happens to that map will happen here. First at this northern part of the forest, then spreading to everywhere else."

Jess nodded angrily. "Come on, we have to grab that map back!"

They dashed across the stage and snatched at the map. Grizelda screeched with laughter and flung it into the air.

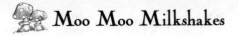 

Puff blew the map high into the air.
With another huge blow, he sent it
swooping through the curtain of vines. He
followed it outside, dancing on the wind
and whistling.

Grizelda laughed. "Friendship Forest
will soon be too horrible for the animals.
They'll all have to leave. Then the forest
will be mine! Ha!"

She snapped her fingers and
disappeared in a spatter of stinking sparks.

The girls heard a loud sob from behind
the curtain. There they found Daisy
Tappytoes, her eyes filled with tears.

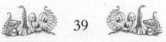

"The map's gone and Friendship Forest will never be beautiful again," Daisy sobbed.

Jess found a tissue in her pocket and gently dabbed the fawn's tears. "Don't worry," she said. "We'll get that map and find a way to put it right."

"We promise," said Lily. "Then the forest will go back to normal."

"We'd better get going before Puff blows the map too far away," Goldie said anxiously.

They jumped off the stage, but Daisy called, "Wait!" and leapt down beside

 40

them. "I want to help," she pleaded.

Lily and Jess looked over to Mr and Mrs Tappytoes, who were standing by the stage. "Is it all right if Daisy comes?" Lily asked them.

The two deer glanced at each other.

"Daisy won't be able to concentrate on anything until the map's found," said Mr Tappytoes. "If you'll look after her, she can go."

"We will!" said Jess.

"We promise," Lily added.

Daisy danced a few tappity steps, then skipped outside, followed by Jess, Lily and Goldie. "Which way?" she asked.

Lily thought for a moment. "Puff went away on the wind," she said, "so let's go the way the wind's blowing."

They set off through the forest,

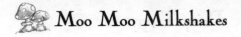 

following the direction of wind and stepping carefully. Thorny vines crawled and twisted around trees and over cottages. Dollops of evil-smelling muck were splattered over flowers and bushes. A creeper had actually pushed through the door of a brightly painted den, and a clear rippling stream was brown and sluggish where it was almost blocked up by Grizelda's muck.

Suddenly Jess stopped. "What's that?" she said, pointing to an animal that seemed to float above a copse of apple trees. It was a smiling, honey-coloured

cow wearing a pink straw hat with strawberries round it.

"A flying cow?" Lily said, astonished.

Daisy giggled. "Come and see!"

They followed her to a small clearing and burst out laughing. The cow was made of painted wood. And it wasn't floating over the trees! It was fixed above the doorway of the Moo Moo Milkshake Hut!

But the hut's walls were grey and crumbly.

"Something's wrong," said Daisy, her smile fading. "The hut's usually the colour

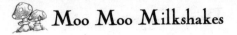 

of ripe bananas."

"It must be Grizelda's horrible spell at work," said Jess.

"I hope Mrs Buttercream the cow is all right," said Daisy. "She planned to make milkshakes for everyone after the show."

Suddenly, a dark vine snaked up the wall, gripped the wooden cow's leg and pulled it over with a crash.

There was a terrified moo from inside.

"Mrs Buttercream!" cried Daisy.

"Let's see if she's OK!" said Jess, and she opened the door.

Daisy ran to hug Mrs Buttercream,

who was behind the counter, looking scared. Frightened animals huddled together beneath a corner table, but a small green duckling crept out.

"Ellie Featherbill," cried Lily, hurrying to comfort her. "What's happened to your feathers?"

"I was drinking my milkshake, and my feathers turned green," quacked Ellie. "Oh no!" She turned to show them her tail feathers, which were red. "I'm changing colour again!"

Poppy Muddlepup appeared from beneath the table. She had shrunk to half

 46

her normal size.

"We were going to go to Harmony Hall as soon as we'd finished our milkshakes," Poppy said in a trembling voice. "Then this happened."

"Look at poor Anna," Mrs Buttercream mooed.

The friends peered beneath the table. Anna Fluffyfoot the kitten was scratching her front, and rubbing her back against a chair leg. "I'm so itchy!" she cried.

The girls gasped. Anna's fur was covered in red splotches.

"Did that start when you drank your

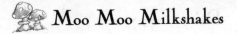 

milkshake?" Jess asked.

Anna nodded and scratched her tail.

"Grizelda's spell must have turned the milkshakes into horrible potions," said Jess.

"Don't worry," said Lily. "We'll put things right ... somehow. Just don't drink any more!"

The friends ran outside and saw a new sign had appeared on the roof:

"You were right, Jess," said Lily. She glanced anxiously at the others. "If we don't break Grizelda's spell," she said, "the whole forest will turn witchy. Who knows what she'll turn the Toadstool Café into? Or Sapphire Lake! Or the Friendship Tree! Or everything else, for that matter. We must hurry!"

They couldn't let that horrible witch ruin the most beautiful place they'd ever seen.

## CHAPTER FOUR

# A Whistling Competition

"Which way?" Goldie asked the others. "Puff and the map could be anywhere."

"Let's split up and search," Daisy suggested.

"No," said Jess, "we promised to look after you. We're staying together."

"But there isn't time to search the whole forest," said Goldie.

Lily peered through the trees, but Grizelda's prickly vines blocked her view. "I don't know how we'll ever find a sprite when we can't see more than a little way," she said.

Daisy's head drooped. She looked so downcast that Jess put her arms around the fawn's soft neck and hugged her.

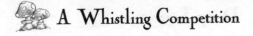 

Then Lily had an idea. "I know! If we can't find Puff, maybe we can get him to find us!"

Daisy looked up with hope-filled eyes. "How?"

"Remember how proud Puff was of his whistling?"

Goldie nodded. "He thinks he's the best whistler ever."

"Exactly!" said Lily. "So if we find a louder whistler, he'll want to prove he's the loudest, won't he?"

Daisy skipped in delight, but Goldie looked worried. She asked, "Who or what

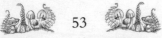

has a louder whistle than Puff?"

"A whistling kettle?" suggested Lily.

Daisy shook her head. "We've got one at home. It's not very loud," she said. "I know – the whistling tree! Its flowers whistle when the wind blows."

"Great idea," said Goldie, "but it's probably covered in Grizelda's creepers."

"We need something that moves," said Jess, "so vines won't have grown over it."

"How about the train?!" Lily cried. "The one that took us to Magic Mountain! That has a loud whistle!"

"Brilliant!" said Jess. "OK, let's walk

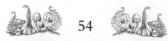

54

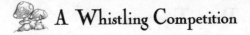 

towards the station and talk about it, at the tops of our voices, so Puff hears!"

As they set off, Lily bellowed, "Puff thinks he's the loudest whistler in the forest."

Jess laughed. "He hasn't heard the train!"

"No," shouted Goldie. "That whistle is much louder than Puff's."

They paused, listening.

Lily noticed that the wind seemed stronger.

"I think he's coming," she whispered, then raised her voice. "Yes, Puff's whistle isn't nearly so loud."

There was a jangling sound behind them. The friends spun around. Two large eyes looked at them from a nearby clump of jingle jangle bluebells.

"He's here!" Lily whispered. "And he's got the map."

"Perfect!" Jess whispered back. "Now let's make sure we get it back!"

Puff puffed out his cheeks and blew.

*Wheeeee!*

Jess cupped a hand to her ear. "Can you hear something?" she asked. "Something really, really quiet?"

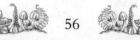

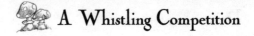 

Lily nodded. "I think Puff is trying to whistle – but we can hardly hear him!"

The sprite leapt on to the breeze and zipped towards them, clutching the map.

"You can hear me! I'm really loud!"

The friends glanced at each other and shook their heads. "I don't think you are," said Lily.

"Me neither," agreed Jess.

"We're not going to hear any loud whistling here," said Goldie, with a wink. "Let's get on the train."

"Wait!" cried Puff. He jumped in front of them. "I'll prove it! I'll prove I'm the loudest whistler ever!"

"OK," said Lily. "We'll have a whistling competition. If the train's whistle is louder than yours, the train wins."

"And if it wins, you must give us that map," said Jess. "Agreed?"

Puff's face screwed up as he thought. Then he nodded. "Agreed," he said. "But

58

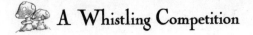 

if I win, you have to tell everyone I'm the best whistler in the forest!"

"It's a deal," said Lily, shaking the sprite's small hand.

Goldie, Daisy and the girls headed for the railway station. They twisted and turned as they struggled through thorny vines, trying not to step in muck.

"It's spreading outside of the northern part of the forest," said Goldie, frowning.

Lily and Jess looked at each other sadly. Soon the whole forest would be witchy and horrible. Meanwhile, Puff rode the breeze above them.

The tomato-red train puffed clouds of
pink steam into the air. A pug dog leaned
out of the cab with a mug in one hand.
He wore goggles and a hat with 'Driver'
written on the front.

"Hello, Mr Whistlenose," said Goldie.

"Hello!" said the dog. "I'm just finishing
my blackberry tea. I needed a break after
cleaning lots of very strange muck off my
train."

Jess quickly explained the problem.

"Please could you make the train whistle as loudly as possible?" asked Lily.

"Anything to help you girls," Mr Whistlenose said. "Daisy, would you like to do it?"

"Yes, please!" she said.

Mr Whistlenose made room in his cab for the excited fawn, and Lily helped her up. Then he showed Daisy where the whistle's pull-chain was.

"Puff, you whistle first," said Jess. "Mr

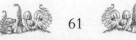

Whistlenose can judge who's loudest."

The sprite's eyes grew enormous and his cheeks bulged as he whistled.

*Wheeeee!*

It was so loud that everyone jumped.

"Well done, Puff," said Lily. "Now it's the train's turn."

Daisy pulled the whistle's chain.

*Peeeeeeeppp!*

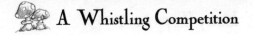 

Everyone, even Puff, clapped their hands over their ears!

Mr Whistlenose declared, "The train wins!"

"Sorry, Puff. That means you lose," said Jess. "Hand over the map."

The sprite flung the map down crossly. "Not fair!" he shouted, as he leaped into the air. The breeze carried him to a twisty willow tree.

"Hooray!" Lily cried, snatching up the map before it could blow away again. "Now we can erase the horrible stuff Grizelda drew!"

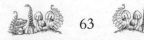

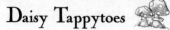

Friendship
Forest would be
fixed in no time.

CHAPTER FIVE

# Scribble Thicket

"Jess, is there an eraser on your pencil?"
Lily asked.

Jess nodded and fished in the pocket
where she carried her little sketchbook
and pencil. She began to rub at Grizelda's
horrible scrawls.

A moment later, she wailed, "Oh no!"

Lily peered over her shoulder. None of the witch's scribbles had been rubbed out.

"My eraser doesn't work on magical drawings!" said Jess.

"If we can't rub it out," said Lily, "the vines and muck will stay, and who knows what will happen to our friends at the Moo Moo Milkshake Hut!"

Daisy's eyes filled with tears.

"To clean a magical map we need a magical eraser," said Goldie thoughtfully. Then she gasped. "A magical eraser – of course!" she said. "There's a glade in the forest called Scribble Thicket," she explained to the girls. "It's full of magical stationery! There are pencil pine trees, notebook bushes, postcard pansies, glue vines – and the rubber tree grows magical erasers!"

"Wowee!" cried Daisy.

"How do we get there?" asked Lily.

There was a bark of laughter behind

them. "On my

train, of course," said Mr Whistlenose.

"Next stop, Stationery Station!"

Puff jumped from the twisty willow on

to the wind and slid towards them like a

surfer. "Haf haf! The train may whistle

louder than me, but I'm faster. I'll beat

you there! I'll pick all the erasers so you

can never fix that map!"

He zoomed away.

Lily grabbed a carriage door handle.

"Hurry, Mr Whistlenose! We must get to

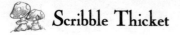 

Scribble Thicket before Puff!"

Mr Whistlenose bounded into his cabin. "Help me shovel magic crystals into the engine," he cried. "That'll make us go extra fast!"

The friends jumped into the cabin. The girls were amazed that there was suddenly room for them all, when there had only been room for Daisy before.

Goldie smiled. "Friendship Forest is full of surprises."

Soon the friends were feeding scoops of magic crystals into the engine's stove. As the crystals landed, they shattered into tiny shards, sparkling and twinkling like a diamond-studded sky.

*Peeeep!*

They chuffed along the track at top speed. One of the pink steam puffballs that rose from the funnel bobbed into the cab. Jess caught it. "Candyfloss for everyone!" she said, offering around delicious handfuls.

In about ten minutes, they drew into Stationery Station. Scribble Thicket was right next to it.

Jess jumped out of the train and ran to the field. "Look! Colouring pencils!" she said, heading to a tuft of moss with

pencils sticking up out of it like reeds. She picked one and tried it in her little sketchbook. "Wow – the colour shimmers!" she said.

"Paper poppies!" Daisy cried, showing the others huge bright white flowers, with petals made of drawing paper.

Goldie jumped aside as a thorny vine snaked across the grass. "Grizelda's nasty work has reached here," she said. "We'd better find that rubber tree before it gets strangled by creepers or covered in muck."

The friends had no time to lose.

 72

## CHAPTER SIX

# The Rubber Tree

"What does the rubber tree look like?" asked Daisy.

"It has big thick leaves, with erasers growing from the tips," said Goldie. "Let's spread out and search."

The girls had to concentrate hard because pretty notebooks, springy pencil

 73

toppers and golden bookmarks kept
catching their eyes and distracting them.

Suddenly Daisy cried, "Here's the tree!"

Goldie and the girls joined her by a tall
tree with glossy green leaves, a smooth,
straight trunk and wide roots spreading
out in every direction. Erasers of different
shapes and sizes hung from the leaf tips.
They were all colours of the rainbow
and every now and then silvery sparkles
fell from them, like a sprinkle of magical
raindrops.

"Wow!" said Jess. "They're beautiful.
Let's pick one each. We'll be quicker if we

all rub out together."

Goldie stared upwards. "They're out of my reach," she said, "and the trunk's far too smooth for me to climb."

Lily groaned. "You mean there's no way to get them?"

"There could be," Jess said slowly. "Remember the Whizzy Wings Mr Cleverfeather invented? Perhaps we could borrow them."

"But the vines will grow over everything soon," Daisy said anxiously. She thought for a moment. "Let's shake the tree and see if the erasers drop down."

The girls tried pushing and pulling the tree, but the trunk was too sturdy and didn't move.

Lily tried to leap up and grab at the

lower

branches

but she couldn't

jump high enough. She landed with a

thump on one of the roots.

Jess saw one of the erasers shake a little

bit loose from the tree. "Look!" she cried.

"That one's nearly ready

to drop. Your jump almost

shook it off!"

"Let's all jump," said

Goldie, "and see if that does

the trick."

They all climbed on to the

roots of the tree and started leaping up and down.

A branch above their heads quivered.

*Thump!*

A pink eraser landed on the grass.

"Keep going!!" cried Goldie. "We need three more!"

"But Puff will be here any minute!" Lily reminded them.

"I know what to do," said Daisy. "I can shake the tree much faster by dancing!" Her shiny red shoes

twinkled as she tapped out a dance move on the roots.

*Tap tap tappety tap … tappety tap tap-tap!*

Lily, Jess and Goldie clapped along as Daisy danced more quickly. The branches were shaking wildly now.

*Tap-tap tap-tap tap-tap tap-tap … tappety tap tap-tap!*

As Daisy tapped faster and faster, more erasers hit the ground. *Thump! Thump! Thump!*

Lily picked them up. They felt soft, like marshmallows, and they still dropped tiny sparkles. She stowed them safely in the

pocket of her playsuit.

"Hooray for Daisy!" everyone cheered.

The little fawn bowed but, as she straightened up, she gasped and pointed. Vines were wrapping around the rubber tree like crawling snakes. Daisy had done it just in time.

"Quick! To the train!" cried Jess. "We'll fix the map on the way back."

Lily and Jess grabbed each other's hands and ran. It looked like they would be able to rescue the forest after all.

## CHAPTER SEVEN

# Jellycakes and Fizz

The train hurtled along the track.

*Choofchoofchoofchoofchoof!*

Lily laid the map on a table so they could each work on one quarter. They rubbed and rubbed. Gradually, they erased the horrible vines, thistles and muck that Grizelda had scrawled on the

 81

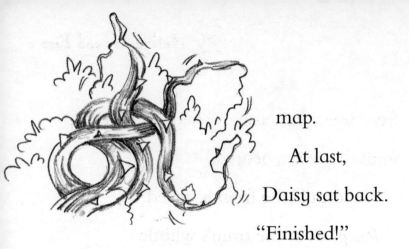

map.

At last,

Daisy sat back.

"Finished!"

"Me, too," said Goldie.

"And me," added Lily.

Jess murmured, "Almost there." Then she sat up, too. "Done!"

Goldie stared out of the window. "It's working!" she cried. "Look!"

Thorny vines were shrinking away

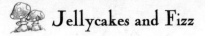 

from trees and bushes. They shrivelled up until they disappeared.

"Hooray!" the friends yelled.

*Peeep!* went the train's whistle.

They passed a rocky, rippling stream. All the sludge that had dirtied the water was disappearing and the stream was turning a sparkling blue.

"We need to celebrate!" said Jess.

A little door, just below the carriage window, slid open. Inside a small cupboard was a plate of tiny strawberry jellycakes, and a jug of frosted pineapple and pear fizz.

"Good old train," said Lily as they helped themselves. "It always knows when you're hungry!"

Soon they chuffed to a stop. The friends thanked Mr Whistlenose and headed back to Harmony Hall.

What a difference they found as they walked through the forest. The trees, bushes and flowers were free of horrible vines, and the paths were clear of prickly thistles and muck. It was all just as it should be.

Right as they reached the curtain of ivy leaves, a voice called, "Daisy!"

 84

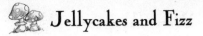 

It was Anna Fluffyfoot, looking happy, and not scratching. Behind her were Ellie Featherbill with her lovely feathers as yellow as they should be, and Poppy Muddlepup, who was back to her proper size.

"The Moo Moo Milkshake Hut is back to normal," said Anna. "Mr Cleverfeather sent Mrs Buttercream his newest invention – the Pully-Pushy. It pulled the wooden calf into place, then pushed it upright, so everything's perfect again!"

"That's brilliant," said Lily, with her arms around Daisy and Anna. "Now we

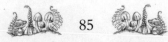

can sit down and relax!"

Jess drew a sharp breath. "Not just yet –
look!"

They all looked round to where Jess
was pointing. An orb of dirty yellow light
floated into the clearing. It exploded into

a storm of smelly
sparks and there
stood Grizelda.
Her face was
purple with fury
and her green
hair was tying
itself in knots.

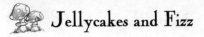 

"Horrible girls!" she screeched. "Nasty animals! You've undone my brilliant spell. Where are my prickly vines and thistles? Where's my sludgy muck?"

Jess stepped forward and yelled, "It's gone, Grizelda!"

"So leave the animals alone!" Lily shouted.

The witch stamped her spike-heeled boots. "What have you done with my stupid wind sprite?" She looked over the girls' shoulders and pointed a knobbly finger. "There he is!"

Jess and Lily turned to see Puff flying

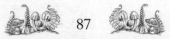

into the clearing and flopping down on his back, panting. He was huffing and puffing hard after trying to keep up with the friends.

Grizelda stalked over to him. "What have you got to say for yourself?"

The sprite shook his head. He was too puffed to speak.

Grizelda scooped him up and stuffed him back in her bottle. He shrank and shrank until all the girls could see was his sad blue face with its big shiny eyes, pressed against the glass.

Jess and Lily glanced at each other.

 88

Both had the same thought. The wind sprites had caused a lot of trouble, but no one deserved to be trapped in a jar.

Grizelda snapped her fingers and shrieked, "I'll be back! I've got two more sprites, and they'll make my plan work. You'll see!"

She vanished in a shower of stinking sparks.

Lily, Jess and Goldie returned the map and Daisy safely to her parents, who couldn't thank them enough. "You've saved our forest," said Mrs Tappytoes.

Jess grinned. "We couldn't have done it without Daisy."

"That's right," said Lily. "Her tap dancing skills brought magical erasers down from the rubber tree. She saved the day!"

Goldie smiled. "Speaking of dancing," she said, "now everything's back to normal, the musical can go ahead!"

"Wowee!" cried Daisy. "I'm off to get ready." She danced a few clickety steps. "Then it's on with the show!"

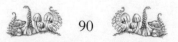

## CHAPTER EIGHT

# Daisy Dances

Harmony Hall glowed pink in the sunshine and the microphone was a glorious marigold again. The animals fidgeted excitedly, waiting for the first act.

Jess and Lily were surprised when Melody Sweetsong the nightingale opened the show instead of Daisy. But

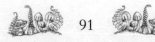

everyone hushed as Melody's beautiful voice filled the theatre, and she finished to cheers and applause.

Next, a very tall animal in a dark blue cloak and hood recited a funny poem along with a very small mouse. It was called "Tiny and Tall Lived Each Side of a Wall." Jess and Lily couldn't see their face, so they weren't sure who the tall animal was.

"I've never seen a giraffe in Friendship Forest," whispered Lily, "so it can't be that."

When the poem ended, the animal took

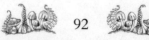

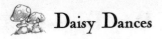

off the cloak. It wasn't one animal – it was two! Lottie Littlestripe the badger was balancing on the shoulders of Great Uncle Greybear, the oldest animal in Friendship Forest!

"Bravo!" everyone cheered.

There were lots more songs, followed by a lively acrobatics routine from Rusty and Ruby Fuzzybrush the fox cubs.

Jess frowned. "Daisy hasn't been on yet," she said. "I hope she's OK."

Olivia Nibblesqueak the hamster gazed up at Jess. "Can I come up, please?"

Jess lifted Olivia on to her shoulder so she could see better.

"I've got a great view from here," squeaked the little hamster. "Daisy didn't go first because she's working out a new dance. I can't wait to see it."

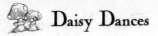 

Just then, Agatha Glitterwing the

magpie perched on the Marigold

Microphone, and a group of animals

gathered with Daisy at the back of the

stage.

Lily whispered to Jess, "It's Anna, Ellie

and Poppy."

Agatha thrust out a wing. "We now

present ... Daisy Tappytoes and Friends

with ... 'The Dance of the Magical Map.'

Daisy ... Tappytoes!"

To Jess and Lily's amazement, the little

fawn danced the story of their adventure,

using nothing more than a scrap of tissue

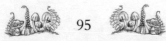

paper, a marshmallow and her own little tappy hooves. Her friends danced in time behind her and made sound effects.

"Choof! Choof! Choof!" they chanted as Daisy pretended to board a train.

"Peep! Peep! Peep!" they piped as she pretended to pull the whistle.

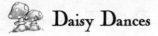 

Daisy tapped out her rubber tree dance, then her friends went "Swish! Swish! Swish!" as she acted out erasing marks on the map.

Finally, she did a happy tappy dance as her friends sang,

*"The forest's looking lovely*
*'Cause Goldie, Lily and Jess,*
*With help from Daisy Tappytoes,*
*Erased Grizelda's mess."*

The curtain came down. The audience stood, yelling "Hooray!" When the curtain rose up again, to reveal all the performers gathered on the stage, many

of them threw flowers to Daisy. But
instead of taking a bow, the fawn skipped
into the audience. To Jess, Goldie and
Lily's surprise, she danced behind them,
shepherding them on to the stage.

"Hooray for Daisy! Hooray for Goldie!
Hooray for Lily and Jess!" the audience
cheered as Daisy, Goldie and the girls
laughed and bowed.

Mr Tappytoes went to the microphone.
"Everyone back to the Moo Moo
Milkshake Hut! It's time to celebrate!"

Mrs Buttercream was making delicious

shakes for everyone. "What would you like, girls?" she asked Jess and Lily.

"They all look scrummy," said Jess. "You choose!"

Mrs Buttercream quickly produced two tall milkshakes that swirled pink and blue. "Two Double Bubbles," she announced.

Jess tried hers. She looked surprised, then giggled. "Ooh! My mouth filled with tiny bubbles," she said. "I felt like I was being tickled!"

The same thing happened to Lily.

Anna grinned. "That's the Double Bubble," she said. "It bubbles in your

mouth, then it bubbles in your tummy and tickles it!"

The girls drank their milkshakes, giggling so much that they made everyone else giggle, too!

Daisy hugged them. "That was such an exciting adventure," she said to the girls.

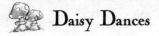 

"It was fun, wasn't it?" said Lily.

"But now it's time for us to go home," Jess said.

Goldie smiled at Daisy's sad face. "Don't worry, the girls will be back soon!"

Jess and Lily said goodbye to their friends, and gave Daisy a special cuddle. "See you soon," they whispered.

Goldie led the girls back to the Friendship Tree. As they reached it, Lily said, "Come and get us if Grizelda starts causing trouble again, won't you?"

"Of course," Goldie said, hugging

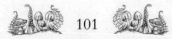

them. "Friendship Forest couldn't manage without you!"

"Thanks for inviting us to Harmony Hall," said Jess. "We saw a great show, and made a lovely new friend."

Goldie touched the tree with her paw. A door opened, spilling out sparkling golden light.

The girls stepped inside. As the light washed over them, they felt the tingle that meant they were returning to their proper size.

When the light faded, they stepped out into Brightley Meadow. Lily grabbed Jess's

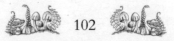

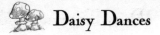 

hand. "Let's see how that woodpecker's doing!"

The two friends skipped over the stream to the aviary at Helping Paw. All the birds were singing, and a starling sat in a nearby tree, whistling sweetly.

"I wonder where that starling learned to whistle? He sounds like Puff!" said Jess.

*Tap tap tap tap tap!*

Lily grinned. "And the woodpecker sounds just like Daisy!"

Mrs Hart stepped out of the barn at that moment. "Hey, you two," she said. "Listen to that birdsong. It's magical – just as if they're putting on a show for us!"

Lily and Jess shared a smile. It reminded them of another, secret magical show!

The End

Lily and Jess are having a wonderful time in Friendship Forest – until horrible Grizelda turns up! The wicked witch unleashes wind sprites to spread havoc throughout the enchanted land.

Can the girls help cuddlesome wallaby Polly Bobblehop bring peace back to her world?
Find out in the next Magic Animal Friends book,

# Polly Bobblehop Makes a Mess

Turn over for a sneak peek ...

Lily and her best friend Jess Forester were in Jess's kitchen. They were making a surprise birthday cake for Lily's mother.

"Dad can put it in the oven for us when it's ready to bake," replied Jess.

"And we'll cover it in candles and sugar roses and give it to Mum when it's finished!" said Lily.

Jess and her dad lived in a cottage opposite Lily's house, where Mr and Mrs Hart ran the Helping Paw Wildlife Hospital. The two vets had set up the hospital in their garden and never turned a sick animal away. Lily and Jess loved

helping with the little patients whenever
they could.

"Miaow!"

Pixie, Jess's kitten, suddenly sprang on to
the counter The tiny tabby didn't see the
cake bowl. She skidded straight into the
side of the bowl and it tipped over! Batter
splattered all over the counter and all over
her fur – right to the white tip of her tail.

"What a mess!" gasped Jess as Pixie's
cheeky yellow eyes peeked out from
under the mixture. "But she looks so
funny!"

"And so adorable," giggled Lily.

Jess started wiping the mixture off Pixie before the mischievous kitten could eat it.

Pixie wriggled from her grasp and ran to the window.

"What is it, Pixie?" asked Jess. She saw something moving outside and gave a gasp of delight. "Look, Lily!"

A beautiful golden-haired cat leapt on to the sill and pawed at the glass.

"Goldie!" exclaimed Lily.

"She must want us to go to Friendship Forest!" breathed Jess. She hung up her apron. "Come on!"

Whenever Goldie appeared, Lily and

Jess knew they were going on a magical adventure. Friendship Forest was a secret place full of adorable little woodland creatures who lived in wonderful homes among the trees. And – best of all – they could talk!

Read

# Polly Bobblehop Makes a Mess

to find out what happens next!

# Magic
## Animal Friends

Can Jess and Lily save the magic of
Friendship Forest from Grizelda?
Read all of series eight to find out!

3 stories
in 1!

www.magicanimalfriends.com